Why Are You Always Following Me?

by Jennifer Licate

Illustrated by Suzanne Beaky

BOYS TOWN Press

Boys Town, Nebraska

Why Is Drama Always Following Me?
Text and Illustrations Copyright © 2022 by Father Flanagan's Boys' Home
ISBN: 978-1-944882-94-5

Published by Boys Town Press, 13603 Flanagan Blvd., Boys Town, NE 68010

All rights reserved under International and Pan-American Copyright Conventions. Unless otherwise noted, no part of this book may be reproduced, stored in a retrieval system, or transmitted in any form or by any means, electronic, mechanical, photocopying, recording or otherwise, without express written permission of the publisher, except for brief quotations or critical reviews.

For a Boys Town Press catalog, call **1-800-282-6657**
or visit our website: **BoysTownPress.org**

Publisher's Cataloging-in-Publication Data

Names: Licate, Jennifer, author. | Beaky, Suzanne, 1971- illustrator.

Title: Why is drama always following me? / by Jennifer Licate ; illustrated by Suzanne Beaky.

Description: Boys Town Press, [2022] | Series: Navigating friendships. | Accompanied by: Why Is Drama Always Following Me? Teacher and Counselor Activity Guide. | Audience: Grades 4-8. Identifiers: ISBN: 978-1-944882-94-5 (book) | 978-1-944882-95-2 (Teacher guide)

Subjects: LCSH: LCSH: Interpersonal relations in children--Juvenile fiction. | Interpersonal communication in children--Juvenile fiction. | Friendship--Juvenile fiction. | Sisters--Juvenile fiction. | Truthfulness and falsehood--Juvenile fiction. | Interruption (Psychology)--Juvenile fiction. | Emotions in children--Juvenile fiction. | Self-esteem in children--Juvenile fiction. | Children-- Life skills guides--Juvenile fiction. | CYAC: Interpersonal relations--Fiction. | Interpersonal communication--Fiction. | Friendship--Fiction. | Sisters--Fiction. | Honesty--Fiction. | Emotions--Fiction. | Self-esteem--Fiction. | Conduct of life--Fiction. | BISAC: JUVENILE FICTION / Social Themes / Emotions & Feelings. | JUVENILE FICTION / Social Themes / Friendship. | JUVENILE FICTION / Social Themes / Self-Esteem & Self-Reliance. | EDUCATION / Counseling / Crisis Management. | EDUCATION / Counseling / General.

Classification: LCC: PZ7.1.L5297 W59 2022 | DDC: [Fic]--23

Printed in the United States
10 9 8 7 6 5 4 3 2 1

Boys Town Press is the publishing division of Boys Town, a national organization serving children and families.

To Elianna and Vinny who are my forever inspiration and to my mom for being my forever support

Chapter 1

I'M ISABEL, BUT MOST PEOPLE CALL ME IZZY. I HAVE A LOT GOING FOR ME, OR SO EVERYONE SAYS. I get pretty good grades, mostly because I finish all my assignments and try as hard as I can. I care about my grades and feel good about myself when I do well. It makes my parents proud of me, too, and I like that.

I play the trumpet in the school band and play on the basketball team. Doing well in my extracurriculars makes me feel good about myself. Basketball and band are fun, and I've met some cool kids doing both, but I don't really hang out with them otherwise. Most of my close friends don't do the same activities as I do.

My friend group is pretty much the same one I've had since first grade, which feels like forever, now that we're in fifth. Unfortunately, lately, it seems like my friendships have changed. I'M WITH MY FRIEND GROUP AND DOING THE SAME ACTIVITIES BUT I FEEL LIKE I'M ON THE OUTSIDE.

Sometimes they share inside jokes that I'm not included in. Would they even notice if I wasn't around? I'm always the last one to hear about get togethers, when it seems like the other girls have known about the plan for days. It makes me sad. What am I doing wrong? It didn't used to feel this way. Maybe they hope I won't come. Maybe they want to do stuff without me.

I wish I felt like I belonged or my friends acted happier to see me. But I haven't felt that way for the past few months. No matter what I do, there's always drama or arguments. I don't feel like I'm rude to my friends but I'm always in the middle of a mess where they say rude things to me or about my opinions. I feel ganged up on. And it feels like it's only me, I don't see anyone else being ganged up on.

I don't know how to avoid arguing because I have to stick up for myself. I like sharing my opinions and talking things out. I'm not rude, just honest. Sometimes that makes my friends mad, and they tell me I'm wrong. When they dismiss me like that, it pushes my buttons.

Then I try even harder to prove my point. If they're my friends, they should want me to be honest with them, right? Otherwise, I'd never say anything. DON'T THEY WANT ME TO BE MYSELF?

I DON'T KNOW HOW TO MAKE MY FRIENDSHIPS BETTER SO WE CAN ALL GET ALONG AGAIN AND HAVE FUN.

Chapter 2

ALL THE ARGUING AMONG MY FRIENDS REALLY BOTHERS ME. MAYBE I SHOULD CHILL WITH THE BAND KIDS OR MY BASKETBALL TEAMMATES FOR A WHILE AND GET AWAY FROM ALL THE DRAMA. Trouble is, I've only hung out with those kids in the band room or in the gym. If we're not making music or playing sports, would we even have anything in common? Would it be fun to hang out with them? Would they want to hang out with me?

Maybe I'm the problem. Maybe I have trouble making friends and getting along with people. What am I doing that makes my friends want to jump down my throat, be rude, and disrespect me?

I have to stop thinking about my friendship problems and pay attention. Mr. Winters, my Language Arts teacher, is quizzing the class on our homework assignment. We were supposed to have finished another chapter last night.

"Who can tell me what the main characters did in chapter five?" he asked. Mari raised her hand super-fast and aggressive-like, convinced her answer was correct.

"The kids ran away," she said smugly.

I couldn't resist correcting her on the spot.

"They weren't running away, Mari. They were allowed to explore."

Mari didn't appreciate being corrected by me. She stared me down and said, "I was just answering Mr. Winters' question, Izzy! Do you always have to disagree with me?"

Here we go again! Another argument. This is so frustrating.

I was just sharing my opinion! Mari gave her opinion, why can't I give mine? I'm not going to let her have the last word.

"Why do you always have to get so sassy with me, Mari? I was answering the question, too!"

Sensing that we were ready to start yelling at each other, Mr. Winters quickly shut us down.

"Okay, Izzy and Mari, there are a lot of ways to view what the characters were doing. Let's talk about it respectfully."

I crossed my arms and said nothing more. I knew I'd get in trouble if I opened my mouth again. I COULDN'T BELIEVE I GOT IN ANOTHER ARGUMENT IN CLASS. AND WITH MARI. UGH!

We'd still be screaming at each other if Mr. Winters hadn't stepped in. But I was just giving my opinion, and Mari jumped all over me. She was wrong! Should I have kept quiet and let her think she was right?

I tried to forget about the argument and just focus on the independent writing assignment, but I overheard Mari say my name to Keisha. Mari's mad at me over a tiny disagreement! I knew she would be! Why can't I give my opinion, too? Because it's different from hers? She was wrong! If Mr. Winters hadn't stopped the class discussion, I would have been proven right.

Mari was talking in a low whisper, so I couldn't hear everything she said, but I clearly heard the words "some people are sooo annoying!" She said that loud, so I would hear her.

"STOP TALKING ABOUT ME!" I SNAPPED.

"STOP EAVESDROPPING, IZZY! IT'S NONE OF YOUR BUSINESS!" Mari snapped back.

"You're talking loud enough for me to hear, so I'm not eavesdropping. And you're talking about me, so IT IS my business!"

"WHOA, WHOA, WHOA, WHAT'S HAPPENING HERE?" Mr. Winters shouted, holding his hands up and half-running toward us.

"Mari was talking about me loud enough for anyone to hear. When I told her to stop, she accused me of eavesdropping!"

"You don't know I was talking about you, Izzy! Stop accusing me of things!"

"Okay, girls, let's settle down. Or would you rather sort this out in the principal's office?"

Mari, with her ears and cheeks turning an angry shade of red, shook her head no and turned away. I didn't talk the rest of the class period. When the bell rang, I walked out deflated and alone. This is exactly what I was trying to avoid. Why are my friends always getting into arguments with me? When they're rude to me, I have to defend myself. Mari's supposed to be my friend, but she talked about me behind my back. She got so mad so fast, she didn't even try to talk to me first or work it out before bad mouthing me to Keisha.

WHAT WAS I SUPPOSED TO DO?

Chapter 3

After school, I was still frustrated and upset about what happened with Mari. I walked home, slammed the front door shut, and threw my bookbag against the wall. All the commotion scared my older sister, Maya, and she screamed, "What's wrong!?" I ignored her and ran to my bedroom.

Moments later Maya knocked on my door and gently asked if she could come in. I waited before answering. I wanted to be left alone, but eventually I told her she could come in. Maya sat down, looking a little freaked out. "What's wrong, sis?"

"As if you really care!"

"Of course I do, Izzy. Sorry if I was kinda rude when you first walked in. I was just so shocked when you slammed the door."

I let out a long sigh and fell backward on the bed. "I got into another fight with one of my friends. This keeps happening!"

"And every time I get into a little argument with one of them, everyone turns against me. No one ever takes my side. Why do my friends always assume it's my fault? They're the ones acting crazy. I'm just sticking up for myself."

Maya wiped away the tears running down my cheeks and wrapped her arms around me.

"Iz, I'm so sorry. Fights with friends can be really hard. Tell me what happened. Maybe I can help."

"I got into a fight with Mari during Language Arts. Our teacher asked us a question about the characters in the book we're reading. Mari said they ran away, which was totally wrong. They were actually exploring, and I said so. That made Mari mad, and she yelled at me in the middle of class… right in front of everyone!"

"Why would that make her mad? Unless… how'd you say it? Were you nice about it and let Mari share her opinion first, or did you jump right in and cut her off when she was talking?"

"I don't know," I admitted. "I think I was respectful. But she WAS wrong." Maya gave me a sisterly smirk, which I didn't need. She knows I hate that.

"Well, Izzy, I know how you can be. When you think you're right, you expect everyone to agree with you. It's great to feel so strongly about things, I guess, but sometimes people aren't gonna agree with you."

I stared at my sister, hurt by what she was saying and trying to understand.

"You wanna make sure you're not squashing other people's opinions just because you don't agree with them. YOU HAVE TO LISTEN TO PEOPLE'S OPINIONS AND IDEAS, EVEN IF THEY'RE DIFFERENT FROM YOURS OR TOTALLY OPPOSITE OF YOURS."

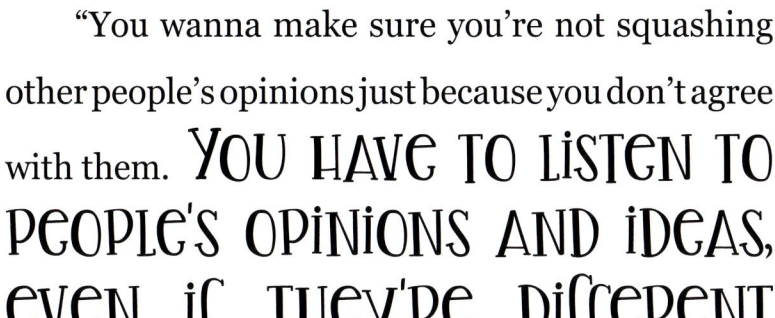

"And yes... sometimes you just need to be quiet when friends disagree with you. Not everything needs to be debated. Sometimes being quiet shows more strength than being loud."

"I thought I was respectful," I said, with more certainty than I actually felt.

"Well, did you let Mari explain what she meant before you jumped in with your opinion?"

"I think so. I think she was done talking."

But as I thought more about it, doubt creeped in. I never thought I talked over people when they shared their opinions, but maybe I do. Even my own sister thinks so. Maybe that's why I've been getting into so many arguments with my friends. I'm making them angry by not respecting their opinions. The thought that all these disagreements might actually be my fault is making me queasy.

"Maya, do you get mad when I cut you off and jump in with my opinions?"

Maya smirked at me again. "Well... you do talk over me a lot, but I usually let it go 'cause you're my baby sister. I know you don't mean to be rude. But your friends probably think you're acting like a know-it-all. Like you don't respect their opinions, and maybe don't respect them."

"But that's not true! I do respect them. If I've been making them feel that way without even knowing it, that's awful."

Maya saw my pain and tried her best to be positive. She said everything would be okay now that I'm aware of how I sometimes come across to others. I just need to make some simple changes, like letting my friends finish talking before I say anything, especially when I disagree with them. More importantly, I shouldn't start needless arguments. Just let others have their opinions and agree to disagree.

I told Maya I could do that. But I still wondered, won't people think I'm being a know-it-all when I do express a different opinion? Maya had advice about that, too. She suggested I soften how I disagree by using phrases, such as, "in my opinion" or "I think." That way I sound more like I'm sharing a thought rather than arguing a point. It sounds nicer, too.

I'm glad I talked things out with Maya. I never knew I was disrespecting my friends' opinions by not listening to them. I probably hurt them even more by demanding they listen to my opinion instead. I wish my friends would've told me how they felt when I talked over them. I thought I was just adding to the conversation by giving my two cents, the same as them. But it must've sounded and felt different. I never wanna make my friends feel like I don't care about their opinions. I know if someone talked over me, I'd think they didn't value my ideas – or me.

I feel guilty and sad for hurting my friends. I care about them and what they have to say. Now I have to prove it.

Chapter 4

I went back to school feeling hopeful and even excited. Now I had a plan to repair my friendships and stop getting into pointless disagreements. Deep down, I knew I had said and did stuff that upset my friends. That's why they didn't always like hanging out with me.

When I saw Mari in Language Arts class, I took a deep breath to calm my nerves.

"Hey Mari," I said in a way that sounded more like a question than a greeting.

"Hey Izzy," she tentatively responded.

"SORRY I WAS KINDA RUDE TO YOU YESTERDAY. I FEEL LIKE I CUT YOU OFF WHEN YOU WERE TALKING."

Mari looked at me strangely. Her expression was a mix of surprise and relief. She probably wasn't expecting an apology, especially from me. Before now, I never knew that talking over someone could be hurtful. And I definitely never ever apologized for doing it.

"It's okay, Izzy. I shouldn't have said anything to Keisha. That was pretty mean of me."

We looked at each other and smiled. Friends again!

I'm glad I apologized to Mari. And it was nice she said sorry to me, too. I didn't expect it. What she said about me to Keisha really hurt my feelings and embarrassed me, but I'm over it now.

Mr. Winters started a discussion about chapter six in our reading book. Some kids had opinions I didn't agree with, but I followed my sister's advice. I didn't talk over anyone.

I raised my hand and waited for Mr. Winters to call on me. I noticed he gave everyone a chance to explain their opinions. THEY WOULDN'T HAVE BEEN ABLE TO DO THAT if I JUMPED IN TO SHARE MY OPINION. I ALSO NOTICED THERE WEREN'T ANY ARGUMENTS, WHICH WAS NICE.

After class, I was feeling pretty proud of myself. Maybe I can do this! I can make changes and get along better with all the kids, but especially my friends. I should be respectful to everyone, just like I want everyone to respect me.

I walked into the cafeteria confident that my friendships were going to get better, and I wouldn't feel so distant from the group. Sitting with my friends, I remembered to do everything my sister said.

I listened and didn't interrupt. It was a blast chatting and giggling with all my friends. Right before lunch ended, everyone started talking about their weekend plans. I didn't have too much going on, just a basketball game, so I listened.

"I'm gonna make cupcakes for my little brother's birthday on Saturday," Tracy said. "I'm making his favorite – chocolate cupcakes with vanilla frosting!"

"Really!" I blurted. "For my sister's birthday, I made all her favorites – lasagna and vanilla cupcakes topped with vanilla frosting." This wasn't exactly true. But it wasn't a complete lie either. Those are her favorite foods, I just didn't make them for her birthday. But I could have, I promised myself I'll do it next year!

"Oh my gosh, Izzy! You're always doing that!" Tracy said, rolling her eyes in disgust.

Then Naomi chimed in. "Yeah, Izzy. Come on, no one even believes you."

I sat there confused. I didn't say anything terrible. But some of the girls shot me dirty looks. Others wouldn't look at me at all. When the bell rang, they packed up their books, ignored me, and walked out of the cafeteria together, leaving me behind. They left me again... I quietly packed up my books.

Now what did I do? They're always getting mad about everything I say. I didn't cut anyone off. I didn't shout at anyone for disagreeing with me. **I JUST JOINED IN THE CONVERSATION! AND IT ENDED IN ANOTHER BIG FIGHT. NOTHING I SAY IS EVER RIGHT!**

Chapter 5

After the argument in the cafeteria, I didn't see my friends the rest of the day. I didn't have a chance to make things better with them – not that I knew how to make things right anyway. I still don't know what I did wrong. I left school in a bad mood - AGAIN! But I wasn't angry like I was after my fight with Mari. Just sad, hurt, and disappointed. What did I do wrong?

As soon as I got home, I dropped my bookbag, leaned against the wall, and slid down to the floor. That's where Maya found me.

"Another bad day, Izzy?" she said. By her tone, I didn't know if my sister was asking a question or stating a fact. Whichever it was, it didn't matter. I was sobbing all the same.

"IT'S POINTLESS! THEY GET MAD AT ME NO MATTER WHAT I DO!"

"Get up and come sit with me. Tell me what happened." Maya held out her hands, pulled me up, and led me to the kitchen table.

"Well... I took your advice and didn't talk over anyone, not once all day."

"OK. SO WHAT'S WRONG?"

"During class, kids were sharing their opinions. Even though I knew they weren't right, I didn't jump in with my own. I let them explain themselves before I raised my hand to answer."

"That's good, Izzy. But you know opinions aren't right or wrong. There can be lots of opinions about one idea or topic. You have your opinion, that you think is right, but others will feel just as strongly that their opinion is right. But still... if you weren't interrupting or cutting people off or telling them they're opinions were wrong, what exactly happened?"

I sat silent for a moment, remembering every detail of what went down in the cafeteria. Slowly, I shared the details with my sister. I described all the fun we were having at the start, before Tracy mentioned how she was going to make birthday cupcakes for her brother. I couldn't look at Maya when I confessed to telling everyone I had made a whole birthday dinner for her.

"IZZY! NO WAY! YOU DID NOT SAY THAT!" MAYA SHRIEKED WITH LAUGHTER.

I wasn't in the mood to be laughed at, but at least my sister wasn't angry at me for lying about her birthday meal that never happened.

"Izzy, you shouldn't say things that aren't true! I'm sure your friends all knew you were lying."

"Maybe. But how would they know? Do you think that's why they got mad?"

"I'm sure that's why," Maya said. "You must have sounded like one of those annoying one-uppers. You know, the kids who are always exaggerating and trying to top anything anyone else says or does."

"That's not a real thing, is it?"

"IT TOTALLY IS! ONE-UPPERS DRIVE EVERYONE NUTS."

"I always assume most of them are either lying or telling half-truths because they're so braggy and saying stuff to always put themselves on top. As soon as a one-upper starts one of their stories, I just roll my eyes and tune out."

Listening to my sister describe one-uppers, I realized why my friends were angry. They thought I was lying to get attention and feel special. And I was, even though I thought I was just adding to the conversation. But what I said wasn't true. My lie took away Tracy's chance to tell us about the special treat she was planning for her brother's birthday. Maya pleaded with me to stop making up stories and one-upping my friends. I promised to do better, but I knew I had a lot to work on if I was going to repair my friendships. I have to stop interrupting and talking over people.

I can't keep telling them their opinions are wrong, and I can't be the girl who's always one-upping her friends. These must be the reasons why I've gotten into so many arguments.

I took all my sister's advice to heart. I paid more attention to how I talked to my friends and classmates. Now when I catch myself falling into old habits, I know how to save myself.

When I interrupt or talk over someone, I apologize and say, "So sorry, were you finished? I didn't mean to cut you off." When I'm being a one-upper, I say with a laugh, "Just kidding. That didn't really happen," and then ask questions to learn more about their experiences.

I'M STILL A WORK IN PROGRESS, BUT MY FRIENDS HAVE ALREADY NOTICED A CHANGE.

I'm not bringing so much drama into our friend group anymore, and everyone is getting along so much better. I don't leave school sad or stressed out about my relationships either. Just today, during lunch, Naomi surprised us by announcing we're all invited to her house for a weekend slumber party.

HOW AWESOME IS THAT?

I feel pretty special being invited. And this time it wasn't one of those "pity" invites that I used to get at the last second because someone felt bad about excluding me. I'm back to feeling like – and believing – I'm really part of the group. When I show up, my friends are excited to see me. And now the only arguing we do is over silly stuff, like what's better... cheese fries or pizza. Definitely cheese fries, I say!

Boys Town Press books
Quick-read chapter books for middle-schoolers

Jennifer Licate
GRADES 4-8

A book series focused on changing friendships, finding your place, advocating for yourself, and being true to who you are.

978-1-944882-63-1
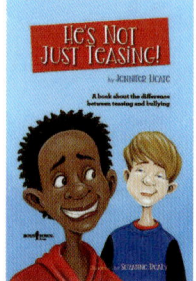

978-1-944882-65-5
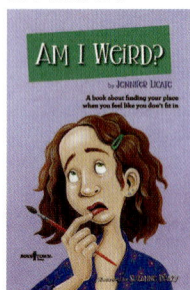

978-1-944882-67-9
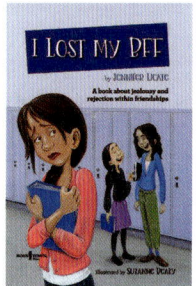

978-1-944882-89-1

978-1-944882-94-5
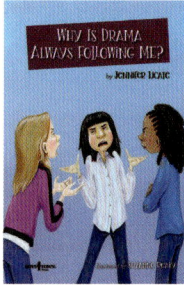

Supplement the learning for each book with its corresponding teacher and counselor activity guide.

A book series teaching important lessons about lying, cheating, and being a good friend.

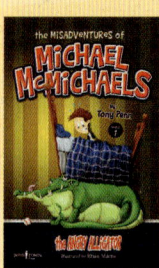
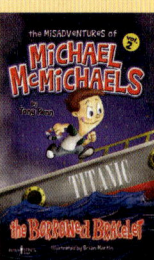
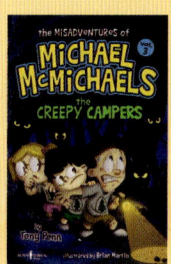
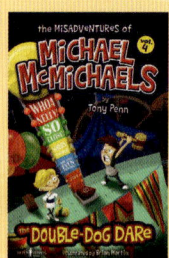
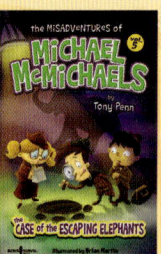

BoysTownPress.org

For information on Boys Town, its Education Model®, Common Sense Parenting®, and training programs:
boystowntraining.org, boystown.org/parenting
training@BoysTown.org, 1-800-545-5771

For parenting and educational books and other resources:
BoysTownPress.org, btpress@BoysTown.org, 1-800-282-6657